Eileen Christelow

THE ROBBERY AT THE DIAMOND DOG DINER

Clarion Books

TICKNOR & FIELDS: A HOUGHTON MIFFLIN COMPANY
New York

MAR 1987

Clarion Books. Ticknor & Fields, a Houghton Mifflin Company. Copyright © 1986 by
Eileen Christelow. All rights reserved. No part of this work may be reproduced or transmit-
ted in any form or by any means, electronic or mechanical, including photocopying and
recording, or by any information storage or retrievel system, except as may be expressly
permitted by the 1976 Copyright Act or in writing by the publisher. Requests for permis-
sion should be addressed in writing to Clarion Books, 52 Vanderbilt Avenue, New York, NY
10017. Printed in Japan. DNP 10 9 8 7 6 5 4 3 2 1 Library of Congress Cataloging-in-
Publication Data. Christelow, Eileen. The robbery at the Diamond Dog Diner. Summary:
Lola Dog doesn't wear her usual diamonds at the Diamond Dog Diner after she hears there
are jewel thieves in town but she doesn't take into account Glenda Feathers' loud talk
about where Lola has hidden her jewels. [1. Robbers and outlaws—Fiction. 2. Dogs—Fiction.
3. Animals—Fiction] I. Title PZ7.C4523Ro 1986 [E] 86-2682 ISBN 0-89919-425-7

There were diamond robbers in town! Glenda Feathers heard the news on the radio just as she was about to deliver her eggs to the Diamond Dog Diner.

"Oh my goodness!" she said. "I must warn Lola and Harry!"

Glenda Feathers rushed into the diner. Lola and Harry were getting ready to open for breakfast.

"Quick, Lola! Hide your diamonds!" Glenda Feathers shouted. "You shouldn't wear them today."

"Why not?" said Lola. "I always wear diamonds when I cook. Otherwise the muffins won't rise and the eggs won't scramble."

"But there are diamond robbers in town!" said Glenda Feathers.

"Oh no!" gasped Lola.

"Don't worry," said Harry. "We'll lock your diamonds in the safe."

"Don't do that!" said Glenda Feathers. "That's the first place a robber would look."

"Do you have a better idea?" asked Harry.

"The eggs," said Glenda Feathers. "Poke a hole in the tops and bottoms of these eggs, blow out the yolks and whites, unstring the diamonds and stick them through the holes…"

"What then?" asked Lola.

"Cover the holes with white glue and put the eggs in the refrigerator," said Glenda Feathers. "No one will ever guess!"

"This sounds like another of your feather-brained ideas," groaned Harry.

"I like it," said Lola.

So the diamonds were safely hidden by the time the first customers arrived for breakfast.

"Now don't tell anyone what we've done," Glenda Feathers whispered to Lola.

Everyone in the diner was talking about the diamond robbers. Someone had heard that they were driving a yellow truck. Someone else had heard that their names were Shorty and Slim and that they were wearing blue knit caps.

"Well, Lola needn't worry," said Glenda Feathers.
"No one will find *her* diamonds."
"Sh-h-h-h-h!" said Harry."
"That's supposed to be a secret!" said Lola.

"Oh, don't be silly," said Glenda Feathers. "Even if someone looks in the refrigerator, they'll never find your diamonds."

Suddenly two customers jumped up from their table and grabbed Harry. One was short and fat. The other was tall and slim. They were both wearing blue knit caps.

"No one move!" they growled. "Just hand over the diamonds."

"*I*...I don't know what you're talking about!" gasped Harry.

"It's the diamond robbers!" squawked Glenda Feathers.

"Let go of my husband," shouted Lola.

The robbers tied everyone up with a long rope. Then they opened the refrigerator.

"But how did they guess?" whispered Glenda Feathers.

"You talk too much," whispered Lola.

"I don't see any diamonds in here," said Shorty.

"Let's just take the refrigerator and get out of here," said his partner. "We can look for the diamonds later."

But when they tried to move the refrigerator, the door swung open. Several eggs fell to the floor.

"Look at this broken egg," said Shorty. "It's got diamonds in it!"

"What kind of bird would lay an egg like that?" Slim whistled.

"The only bird around here is that blabbermouth chicken," said Shorty. "Maybe we should take her with us."

"You've got the wrong idea!" shouted Glenda Feathers as the robbers released her from the rope. "Leave me alone! I don't know anything!"

But Slim carried her, kicking and screaming, out to the yellow truck and Shorty carried a box filled with all of the eggs. They locked the eggs and Glenda Feathers in the back of the truck.

As the truck raced out of the parking lot, Glenda Feathers pounded at the back window.

"Help!" she screamed. "Don't let them take me away!"

Everyone tugged and pulled and chewed at the rope.

But by the time they broke loose, the truck had disappeared.

"What are we going to do!" said Harry. "We may never see Glenda Feathers again!"

"We may never see my diamonds again, either," said Lola. "I just hope Glenda Feathers can think of a way to get out of this mess!"

And that is exactly what Glenda Feathers was trying
to do as she sat tied to a rickety chair in the robbers'
hideout. She watched them break open the eggs.

"What are you going to do with me?" she asked
nervously.

"Shut your beak!" said Slim.

"I wonder why some of these eggs have diamonds in them and some don't," said Shorty.

"Maybe the eggs are from different birds," said Slim. "How do we know we have the right bird?"

That's it! thought Glenda Feathers. *I'll make them think there's another bird*!

"You *don't* have the right bird!" said Glenda Feathers.

"She talks too much!" said Slim. "Stuff her in a sack!"

"I won't say another word," cried Glenda Feathers. "I won't even tell you how to find her!"

"How to find who?" asked Shorty.

"The bird who lays eggs with diamonds in them," said Glenda Feathers.

"You better tell us how to find her, or you'll be a barbequed chicken," said Shorty.

"Oh, no!" shrieked Glenda Feathers. A tear rolled down her cheek. "I...I think she'll deliver her eggs to the diner at dawn tomorrow. But..." she said quickly, "I should call Lola and Harry to make sure."

"It's a trick," said Slim.

"This bird is too dumb to play tricks," said Shorty.

When the phone rang at the Diamond Dog Diner, Harry and Lola answered together.

"Glenda Feathers!" they gasped. "Where are you?"

"Listen carefully!" said Glenda Feathers. "You know that chicken with the diamond eggs?"

"What are you talking about?" said Harry.

"Someone wants to meet her," said Glenda Feathers. "Can you make sure she delivers her eggs *at dawn tomorrow*?"

"I think Glenda Feathers is trying to tell us something," whispered Lola. "Say the chicken will be here."

"But we don't know any other chickens," Harry said
to Lola after he hung up the phone. "So how can we
have a chicken here tomorrow at dawn?"

"You'll see," said Lola.

Early the next morning, before dawn, a yellow truck parked around the corner from the Diamond Dog Diner. Slim and Shorty were in the cab. Glenda Feathers sat tied up between them.

"One cluck from you and it's all over," said Slim.

Just then a strange-looking chicken walked up to the diner with a basket of eggs.

"There she is," whispered Glenda Feathers.

"But that chicken has furry feet," said Slim.

"All diamond-laying chickens do," said Glenda
Feathers.

Slim and Shorty quickly shoved Glenda Feathers
into the back of the truck.

"Aren't you going to let me go?" she asked.

"We'll talk about that later," they said. They locked
the door. Then they followed the chicken into the
darkened diner.

Suddenly the lights went on. Lola and two policemen jumped up from behind the counter.

"We've got you!" they yelled.

The chicken whirled around.
"Surprise!" said Harry as he pulled off his mask.
"We were tricked!" shouted Shorty and Slim.

The policemen handcuffed Shorty and Slim and took them away while Harry and Lola searched the yellow truck for Glenda Feathers.

All they found in the front was a bag of chocolates.

"My favorite kind!" said Lola. She popped several into her mouth. Just then, a faint cry came from the back of the truck.

"It's Glenda Feathers!" said Harry. He and Lola rushed to unlock the back door.

"Am I safe?" cried Glenda Feathers. "Did you catch the robbers?"

"Where are my diamonds?" asked Lola.

"You've already found them," said Glenda Feathers.

"What do you mean?" asked Harry.

"I had another wonderful idea," said Glenda Feathers. "When the robbers wanted to hide the diamonds again, I suggested dipping them in melted chocolate. They're right in that bag!"

"But I just ate some," groaned Lola.

"Oh, dear," said Glenda Feathers. Then she smiled. "Well, at least no robbers will ever find *those* diamonds."